Little Pro Surfer

Henry has been an educator and school administrator for more than 20 years. His passion for helping children inspired him to write children's books with positive meaningful messages. Henry knows kids. In "Little Pro Surfer" he combines his love of surfing and education to instill powerful messages. *"If you can dream it, you can achieve it"*. His hope is to motivate children all over the globe to go after their dreams; not only in surfing but whatever their little hearts desire.

Krush Illustration is the dynamic duo Paulina Michel & Bobby Skelton. Both graduated from Laguna College of Art + Design with BFA's in Illustration. They grew up reading children's books and have never lost the child within. They want to share their passion of art with future generations.

This book is dedicated to my daughters, Pearl and Paulina, who never waiver in pursuit of their passions. Pearl is a gifted musician and Paulina is the best artist I know.

This book was written and illustrated on the island of Kauai.

Little pro surfer, little pro surfer what are you going to do?
I'm going to grow up and make the world tour!

Little pro surfer I'm going to help you!

Everyone tells me that some surfers can grow up to be real poor!

Not everyone makes it on the world tour.

Little pro surfer, little pro surfer it is true but some surfers grow up to be business owners and oceanographers Some might even end up as famous photographers!

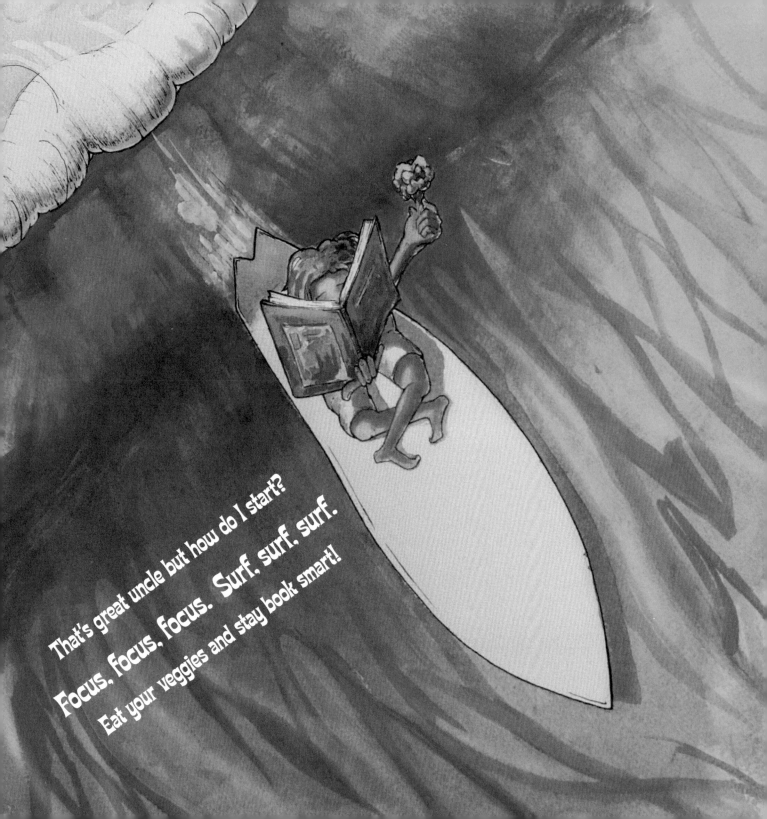

That's great uncle but how do I start?
Focus, focus, focus. Surf, surf, surf.
Eat your veggies and stay book smart!

Uncle, uncle all I want to do is rip, rip rip!
I want to go on many surf trips!

If you can visualize, you can materialize!
If you can dream it, you can achieve it!

Uncle, uncle, what if I get caught in a rip or get carried out to sea?

All the hard work and swimming will make you strong!

You will be confident in the ocean, you will see!

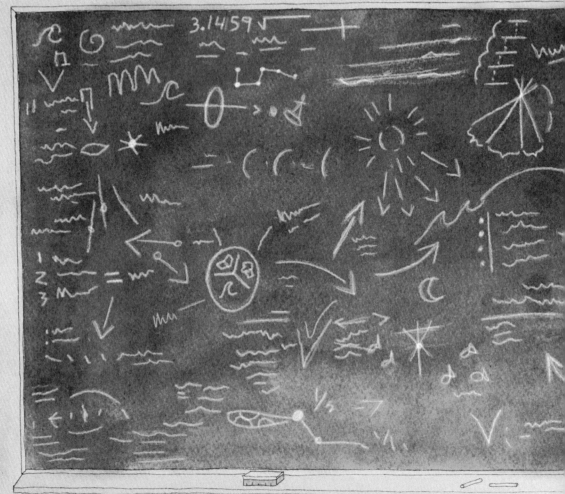

Lil Pro surfer, sometimes we learn more from losing than we do from winning.
Uncle, uncle what do you mean?

It is learning from our mistakes that makes us strong and wise.
Learn from them so you don't make them twice.

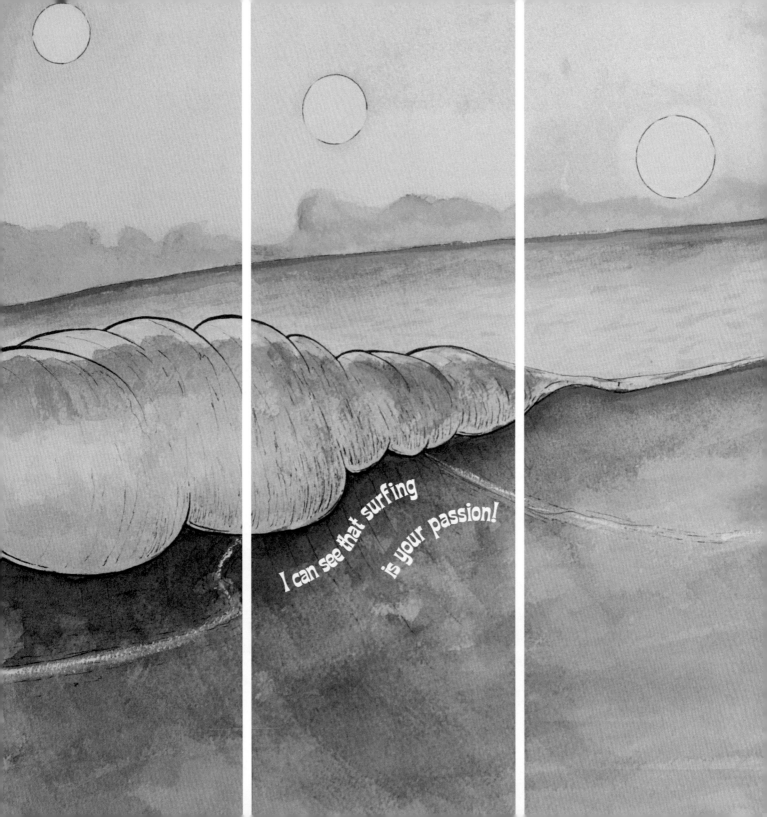

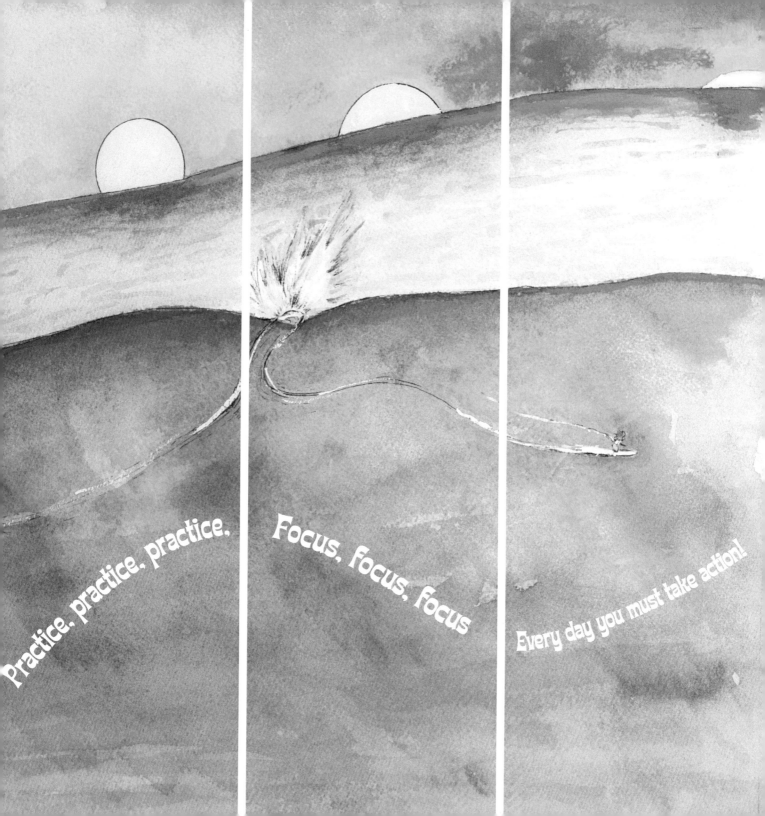

Practice, practice, practice,

Focus, focus, focus

Every day you must take action!

Little pro surfer little pro surfer if you can visualize you can materialize! If you can dream it you can achieve it!

Made in the USA
Middletown, DE
22 September 2016